The Story Setting

THOMAS'S HOUSE

SCHOOL

LIGHTHOUSE

BAILEY BEACH AQUARIUM

DOLPHINS

SEALS

WHALES

PARKING

PARKING

AQUARIUM

HOPS

3

TABLE OF CONTENTS

Two Hours
with Tilly

ALISON PETERS

Illustrated by Ritva Voutila

sundance
A Haights Cross Communications Company

The Story Characters

Thomas

Dad

Tilly

CHAPTER 1

Bailey Beach Aquarium

Thomas decided not to speak to his dad ever again. Not one more word.

"I'll pick you up at four," said Dad.

Thomas said nothing.

"I'm sorry I can't come with you, Thomas. This meeting just came up."

Thomas kept his mouth shut.

"I'll come next time," said his father.

Thomas got out of the car.

"I promise," his dad called to him.

Thomas slammed the car door and walked into the Bailey Beach Aquarium.

Thomas sat on a chair looking at the
vending machine. He had just enough
money for some peanut butter crackers.
If he ate slowly, they would last until
Dad came back. He wasn't interested in
looking at fish. It was no fun alone.

A small girl skipped toward Thomas. She turned to look behind her, as if someone was following her.

She didn't notice Thomas's legs. She tumbled over his shoes.

"Ouch!" cried Thomas. "Watch where you're going."

"E-e-e-e!" the girl laughed. "I'm sorry."

She looked behind her. A man in a white coat came around the corner.

"There he is!" she squealed. "Bye," and she ran away again. Her blue stockings sparkled.

The man scratched his head and looked around. He looked under the chairs. He even looked into the large aquarium in the middle of the room.

He scratched his head again. Then he
turned and walked slowly back the
way he came.

Thomas was fascinated. Was this man
the girl's father? Why was he wearing
a white coat? Were they playing a
game? Thomas and his dad had played
games like that—before mom got sick.

Suddenly Thomas felt like crying, so he closed his eyes. He didn't want to feel sad. He decided to follow the man.

CHAPTER  2

Follow That Girl

The man walked down the corridor. His coat flapped behind him. He met a woman in a white coat.

"She was here again. I'm sure of it," the man said.

"I want to believe you, Jim," said the woman as she opened a door. "But it just sounds so crazy."

"It's true," said Jim. "Somehow I'll find her and prove it."

Thomas wondered what the man wanted to prove.

When the door closed, Thomas read the sign.

Laboratory—Staff Only.

They are scientists, thought Thomas.

Thomas decided to find the girl himself.
He wandered through the corridors.
He searched in front of the seal pool.

He looked around the dolphin pool,
the whale pool, the shark tank—even
the cafe. She was gone!

Thomas stood outside trying to think
of other places she might have gone.
He glanced over at the main building.
He decided to look there again.

CHAPTER 3

Finding Tilly

Thomas stopped in front of the girls' bathroom. No way, he thought. He was not going to look in there.

Suddenly, a tiny voice said, "Hello."

Thomas turned around. It was the girl.

"The boys' bathroom is over there," she giggled.

Thomas's cheeks turned pink.

"I'm not going in. I was just looking." That sounded worse. The tips of his ears felt warm.

"My name is Tilly," said the girl.
"That's short for Matilda, you know."

Thomas thought it was a silly name.
His name was Thomas, not Tommy.

"Why is that man following you?"

"I'm playing a game," she giggled.
"He wants to know my secret."

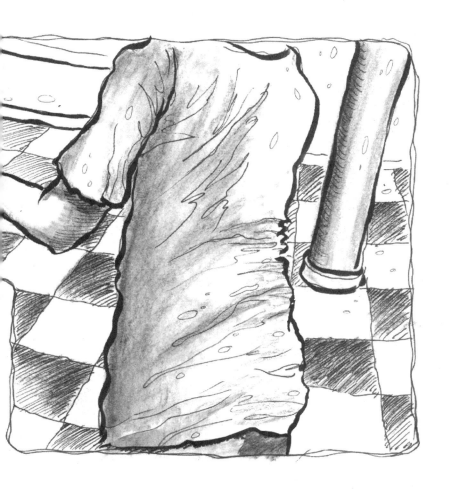

"What is your secret?" asked Thomas.

"Well, Thomas," she whispered as she leaned closer. "I can't tell you," the girl laughed out loud. "It's a secret!"

She said this as if it was a great joke. Thomas didn't think it was funny.

The girl quickly ran down the hall. Her run looked more like a skip. As Thomas watched her go, he tried to remember when he had told her his name.

The Shark Tank

Tilly skipped down the ramp that led to the shark tank. Thomas raced after her.

"Hey," he called. "Hey! How did you know my name?"

"Easy," she said. "I read your mind."

"I don't believe you," said Thomas.

"That's OK," said Tilly, giggling. "Do you want to play a game with me?"

"What's the game?" said Thomas.

Tilly turned to face Thomas.

"Well, the scientist wants to know my secret. He knows I'm different. He thinks that I might be . . . ," her voice became a whisper, ". . . a mermaid."

"There's no such thing as a mermaid."

Tilly smiled. "Really?" she said.
"Maybe you're right, but maybe you're
wrong. Quick, he's coming! Let's go."

She grabbed his hand. She dragged him down to the viewing area that ran around the shark tank.

Tilly skipped along ahead of Thomas until she disappeared into a glass tunnel. It went straight through the bottom of the tank. Tilly went in until she stood in the middle of the tunnel.

SHARKS

She pressed her nose against the glass.
"Hello, my lovelies," she said. "Today
this boy Thomas has joined my game."
She turned to Thomas. "Come closer."

Thomas didn't want to get too close.
He stood behind Tilly.

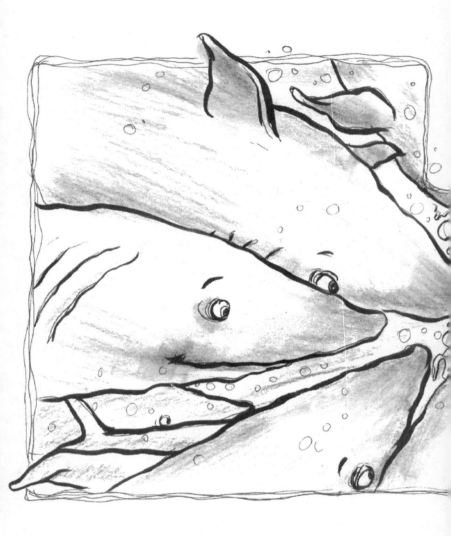

Tilly smiled. She put her nose against
the glass. "It's nice to see you again,
my friends," she whispered.

Then the strangest thing happened. All of the sharks began swimming toward her. Thomas couldn't believe it.

"Uh-oh!" giggled Tilly. "Here comes the man in the white coat. Time to go!"

She grabbed Thomas's hand again and dragged him along. Thomas turned to see the scientist slowly moving in their direction. He was searching for Tilly.

Then the scientist suddenly stopped. He
noticed all of the sharks lined up facing
the tunnel. His eyes grew wide, and he
scratched his head. Then he pulled out
a notebook and began taking notes.

CHAPTER 5

Talking to Whales

Tilly dragged Thomas outside. Out on the deck of the aquarium were three large pools. Tilly ran to the whale pool and leaned over the fence. She closed her eyes and sang hello.

Then it happened again. The two whales swam to the side. They were so close that Thomas could look into their eyes. Something mysterious was going on. He could feel it.

Tilly leaned forward. The ends of her long hair fell into the water and floated on the surface. Then she closed her eyes and started to hum softly.

"There," she whispered. "I'm finished."

"Finished what?"

"Telling them how much I've missed them," said Tilly.

"I don't believe you!" said Thomas.

"That's OK," she laughed. "E-e-e-e-e."

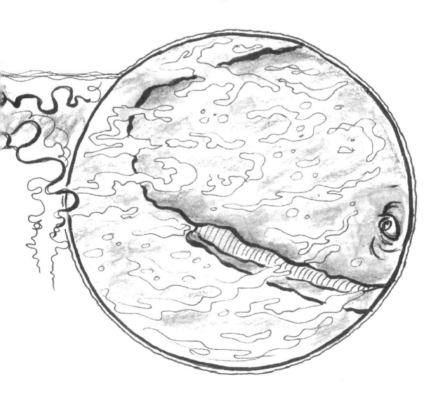

Tilly's laugh was loud. It seemed that
the dolphins had heard her. They began
to make their dolphin sound.

Thomas realized it was exactly the same sound that Tilly made when she laughed! "E-e-e-e-e."

He'd never ever heard a person laugh like that before.

"Why do you laugh so much?"

"Because it's so lovely to laugh up here!" she said. "Where I live, if you laugh too much you might drown."

"Where exactly do you live?"

Tilly frowned for a second. Then she shrugged. "Out there," she said, and pointed to the ocean. "But that's part of the secret."

"Where? Do you live on an island or a boat? And why would you drown if you laughed?" asked Thomas.

"Questions, questions," she giggled. "Because you'd get so much water in your mouth, silly!" Tilly looked over the fence to Bailey Beach.

"High tide," she sighed. "I have to go."

Thomas looked toward the beach, too.
The tide was very high. It came close
to the stone wall that ran along the
beach and went around the aquarium.

He turned back to Tilly, but she was nowhere to be seen. He called out her name, but she did not reply.

CHAPTER 6

She's Gone

"You were with her. Where did she go?" said a low voice beside him.

Thomas turned. He was face to face with the white-coated scientist.

"I don't know," said Thomas.

"Maybe she went inside," said the man.
He dashed back through the doors.

Thomas walked along the beach. Near the wall, he saw a tiny object. It glinted in the sun. He picked it up.

It was a large blue fish scale. He had never seen a scale like it before. He put it in his pocket. Then he walked to the parking lot.

CHAPTER 7

Going Home

"Hello, Thomas," said Dad.

Thomas looked at his dad. His dad looked tired.

"I'm really sorry today didn't work out the way we planned," said Dad. "I'm happy to be with you at last."

Thomas thought about not answering,
about never speaking to his father
again. Then he thought about how
hard his father worked.

"It's OK, Dad," he said, and he meant
it. "Actually I had a good time."

His father smiled. "Great. That's great,"
he said, and he looked relieved.

"Dad?" asked Thomas.

"Yes, Thomas?"

"Are mermaids real?" Thomas asked.

"No, of course not," Dad smiled. "Why do you ask?"

"No reason," he said softly. Thomas felt in his pocket for the smooth scale.

Thomas didn't say anything to his dad, but in his heart he knew. He knew that mermaids were real. He had the proof in his pocket.

GLOSSARY

aquarium
a tank where water
creatures are kept

corridor
hallway

fascinated
very interested or
curious about

laboratory
where scientists work

mermaid
a creature that is
half-woman and half-fish

mysterious
something that seems
secret or strange

tumbled
fell over

vending machine
a machine that you can
buy food and drink from

Talking with the Author and the Illustrator

Alison Peters (author)

What do you like about yourself?
My big feet. They are long, strong, and do what-ever I tell them to.

Why did the cow jump over the moon?
She was in training for a much bigger jump over the sun.

Ritva Voutila (illustrator)

What do you like about yourself?
My skin. It stops me getting too full of myself.

Why did the cow jump over the moon?
Because if it jumped over the sun, it would become barbecued spare-ribs.

Published by Sundance Publishing
P.O. Box 1326, 234 Taylor Street, Littleton, MA 01460
800-343-8204

Copyright © text Alison Peters
Copyright © illustrations Ritva Voutila

First published 1999 as Sparklers by
Blake Education, Locked Bag 2022, Glebe 2037, Australia
Exclusive United States Distribution: Sundance Publishing

ISBN 0–7608–8105–7

Printed in Canada